All The Moon Travellers

Mat de Melo

The original,
unedited poem.
A love letter
to Lisbon.

ISBN 13: 978-1-7322497-3-8

Dedication:

This book is a
dedication to all
the moon travellers,
and to when Lisboa
was Lisboa.

Meta Fiction |n|

A false and usually
improbable account.
An idea or a word,
measured in astronomical
units. May defy certain
conditions, and make
almost anything happen.
i.e. To move or spin
round, as if by magic.
To manufacture,
or color in. A producer

of ideas. A hero in a
novel, on a stage,
in the backdrop
of a motion picture
with a word pad.

All The Moon Travellers

Act 1

The curtain
goes up.

In a café. A girl

in denim with a

memo pad is in the

corner of the room.

I entered the room

like a star in a
50's motion picture.

I sat with Viola
under a delta coffee
poster. I had a cola,
and Viola had a
porto, and together
we sat in a corner
and observed
everything with

hopeful attention
over several minutes.

"I want to paint
the town red. I want
to be on a stage,
and be the part. I
want to bring the
house down."

Viola had an idea.
"We could steal a

Porsche and drive around, and listen to the radio until there's no more gasoline."

Milo unfolds a paper. On it had the words "build me a time machine" in blue ink. A girl in denim blue Levi's and a man in a

plain white t-shirt
and retro aviators,
when every night a
motion picture, and
everyone a star; when
a rocketeer could move
40 thousand miles per
hour through outer
space in the direction
of the Moon or Mars
fastened to his seat;

when America meant
Kodak and milkshakes
and midsummer rides in
the car; when all the
world really was a
stage, and all the men
really players.

"You are a
troublemaker!"

"And you a superhero."

Dissolve to:
In a second-floor
apartment. On a 37
y/o melodramatic
visionary. Near a
kerosene lantern and
a memo on monsters and
nightmares and fiction,
and a certain something
that is the product of
a retroactive mind.

On an obligation;
a universal
responsibility,
and the world
was waiting.

**I dial in on a
static radio
frequency.** On a
carton box, and a
70-word blueprint.

A generation set a
standard: Bring a
disposable camera.
Spin 'round, dial in,
and roll the tape.
A generation of

movers and shakers
develop a philosophy.
A revolution is had.

  Again I had an
impression, in
a second-floor
apartment, burning
the midnight oil.

Everything moved
quickly, and the
odds were nearly
always against us.

And yet, we
insisted, that a
night owl can't
be sleepy at night.

On a red "71" Fiat
Berlina, watching
stars. Milo and Viola
have red wine on the
hood of the car.
Viola has a blue
and red memo pad.
Milo sees the world
in primary colors.

"A poet is no
ordinary person.
He says often somewhat
crazy, not possible
things. He has
the magic marker."

Viola had the
radio, and I
had the marker.
"A flower is a
flower, and a

catcher in the
rye is a catcher
in the rye. An
alternative generation
is ready with
anticipation."

The radio is on.
"Words paint pictures,
and rockets go to
the moon."

A bus rolled in.

"On paper and in
blue ink?"

"He tied a lasso
around it, then
pulled it down from
outer space. It is
in his pocket,
glowing in the dark,
and it is sure to
give him away."

"And then?"

"And then like fiction, a chemical reaction is had, in a boxcar, rounded with a dream."

"Then a user's manual, a *how to make a paper moon*."

Behind us a Roman
Candle exploded.
Viola turned and
paused, and I turned
and paused, like in a
movie I had on tape.

**On boxed wine,
and hyperboles.**
On the 3.70 I had

and saved and

wasted. On 73rd

Street and Broadway,

having a cola.

In Rio and Roma

and Madrid, all

around the world,

taking all the

chances, making

all the mistakes.
A handbook for
idea makers.

In Bairro Alto
with a disposable
camera with 24
exposures and a
blue marker.

A 3100-word
dissertation on
Juno and Mars. On

Eros and arrows and
chemical reactions.

On a buoy marker
with red reflectors
that projected for
many kilometers in
every direction.

Casino Estoril.

I had a gin and
tonic in the bar.
The idea? More info
on the Bright Young
Things in the bar,
and warn the world
of a subculture
of people who rode
into Madrid and Porto
and Rome on a boxcar,
each one a superhero.

They measured the
distance between
them and the moon,
and they calculated
the cost of gasoline;
speed, distance, time.

I imagined an
Overture, act 1.
Pulled in by gravity,
pushed on by my
imagination.

**To a blue and brown
and red backdrop.**
Viola had a generic
cola on the floor
with a memo pad.
I dial in on blue
marker, in a blue
and brown and red
backdrop, laying
the foundation

for a special

school of thought.

On a stage, and

like in a movie

I had on tape.

There is a

generator of ideas.

All in on fiction,

he developed a time

machine. He imagined

a dot on a line in

a map. In Spain,

making no mistake.

  Dissolve to:

Milo in a *basic white*

t-shirt, at his desk

on a portable word

machine. Make an

outline. Use saturated

colors. Don't worry about staying in between the lines. You are here to save the world. It is up to us. Consider this: an idea maker cannot depend on if he is misunderstood, and that to be misunderstood is

also that which
makes us different.

 Red, yellow, blue,
I can see the
billboards from
here. I can see a
moving picture in
the distance. I can
hear the sound of
the words on paper.

I can see the Moon.
I can see a poet
philosopher. I can
see a time machine.
It is there. It is
fiction, and it
is ours to have.

I dial in on a green buoy marker in Cais de Sodre. Viola had a cigarette, and I had a box of matches.

I had a blue Walkman, a retro mixed tape, and me and Viola sat on a box with the phones in our ear, drunk on

an idea I had on a 28
tram. I dial in on a
lighthouse, and then
I paused. " ... I am
a romantic, and a
sentimentalist, and
I hold that though
nothing could last
forever, I know I've
done all I could to
make it so."

"I'd like to think that we could," said a girl in denim blue Levi Strauss. "In a movement named *the manufacturers of ideas*. In an ad, in movie poster words, a tragicomedy. In *cinemas July 13.*

310, 540, and 830."

*Viola has more
red wine. Milo
has a somewhat
novel idea.*
"All I ever wanted
was everything,
but all I ever
had was *fiction*."

*Viola dials in on
an autocarro.*
"And then?"

Milo pauses.
"Let's walk around,
and drink cheap
champagne, and make
trouble, and pretend
like the night'll
last forever."

The *autocarro*
rolls in as Viola
has an idea.
"Act 1, scene 3.
I'll be the hero,
and you be the
narrator."

Nighttime, somewhere in Lisboa. There is a
box of *espumante*.
Viola is on the
floor with a
transistor radio.

I unfold a memorandum:
Madrid, Barcelona, Rome.
Bring a wordpad. Take a
ride, make a mistake.

The Moon is
tangerine, and
nighttime is the
color blue.

"The Moon, the stars.
These mittens. There
is more, and if not
then what is there?"

"There is proof.
There is magic.

The stuff that
words are made of.
On paper there is a
girl in denim on a
10-hour midnight
Renfe from Lisbon
to Madrid, all in on
an idea. Who dreamed
in color. And there
were the words,
La Espera."

I had a bottle of *espumante*. The volume on the radio is on 10, and me and Viola had one toast after another ...., "To you, to me, to us, to the misunderstood," and with every toast we slammed our bottles

together under the
moon in a time machine.

"Good night paper moon.
Goodnight bright light.
Goodnight, goodnight.
Goodnight late-night."

It was only midnight,
but it was always
only midnight to an
intoxicated heart.

So began a different
sort of blueprint;
a novel I had and
erased and erased,
till all I had
left was the poetry
between the lines.

I had an 830-word
dreamer's guide to
the Milky Way, and
good, cheap champagne,

and an 830-word

dreamer's guide

to The Milky Way

and good, cheap

champagne is code for,

"the night is young,

and so are we."

Milo and Viola

climb into a brown

carton box like it

is no ordinary

brown carton box,
and like they are
no ordinary people.

And so, Milo and
Viola had cheap
champagne, and
listened to the
radio, and pretended
like they were in
a movie called
Ultraviolet Blue.

Act 2

A midnight show

Set design: A blue
backdrop, and a
paper star that
Viola colors in.

There is memo
paper on the floor.
There is a typewriter,
and a super 8
projector. There
is a movie poster,
and an am/fm radio.

Fade in on a
movie projector,
and 500 thousand
kilowatts of star

particles. On a
ladder, under a
paper moon.

**A poet has a
color slide,** and
the whole world
in bold, saturated
colors, and without
limit or exception.

Eligible to anyone
with resolution, and
under all conditions.
He considered anything,
and everything as
able to be possible.

A dream is a dream;
a discontinued
crayon, but a
crayon nonetheless.

I dialed in on an
electric tram car.
On a retro Ford van
w/ brown and red and
tangerine lines and
a number 73 glued
on both sides.

I sat on a step by
a theater and read
Babylon Revisited on
The Saturday Evening

Post, and I considered
the idea, a near
impossible idea I had
when I was 10, on *how
words have an effect.*

I dialed in on a
porto wine ad on a
bus. I re-read my
notes, and leaned
back and watched
everything happen.

Dissolve to: A theater

on Dom Pedro. A man

in a wool shirt w/

a violin played *O*

Cisne de Saint Saëns

near a box of flyers.

In a moving picture house. Milo is in seat 3A, and Viola is behind him in 4B. A projector projected a movie on the screen.

Milo turns to Viola with a disposable camera. He wonders if he has time, and if he and Viola

are in a sad
motion picture.

*Cut to: Milo on
stage. A projector
beam is on Viola.*

VIOLA: The curtain
goes up on a girl
in Barcelona. Near
the Teatre Borràs.

Under the moon.
To which we chase
the Nighttime. We
defy what is normal,
and we depart from
the literal use of
words. To color
Everything in.
An almost possible
idea intended to be
taken as verbatim.

Curtain closed.

MILO: Again the
curtain goes up.
On the hero. In a
boxcar. On a stage,
and on fiction:
because that's what
everybody wants; a
time machine, and

that almost possible
feeling like you are
in a motion picture,
and you are in the
middle of your
favorite part.

VIOLA: You are
a god from
the machine.

MILO: The moon, the
stars. Everything.
It is ours to have.

VIOLA: And a romantic.

MILO: ... You are
that which dreams
are made on.

VIOLA: And you are
rounded with a sleep.

MILO: And on a paper moon.

Viola turns to the projector.

VIOLA: I can almost see Barcelona from here. The weight of the Universe. Gravity pulls me in, and somewhere there there's

a goodbye.

Milo has an

antidote.

MILO: Its conquest

deserve the best

of mankind, not

because it is easy,

but because it is

hard. Why the moon?

Why fiction? Because
it is there. Because
words color it in,
and because me are
you are different.

Viola turns
to the screen,
then back again.

VIOLA: Like you
had on tape?

A projector beam is
on Milo. Viola turns
to an empty theater,
and together, Milo and
Viola read lines from
act 2. In a motion
picture, all in on
words on paper.

A bus stop in *Rato*.

I was in an aviator

flight suit, and

Viola was in a

polyester coat.

It began to rain.

I unfolded the

paper in thirds,

then I read the poem

aloud, in an almost

too soft to hear

the words voice.

"'*In defense of*

the misunderstood.

No Barcelona, and no

Miró. No radio, and

no dial. No Billie

Holiday, and no

Harlem dream.

 No retro word

machine, and no buoy

marker on a sound

that projected a
beam of light in
every direction.

No drama, no act 2.
No measure of time,
and no special sense
of urgency only a
dreamer like you and
me could understand.
No guide to the
Milky Way, and no

democratic citizen
publication.

No exaggerated ideas,
and no paper moon.
No movers, and no
shakers. No brown box,
and no rocketeers.
No good, cheap red
wine, and no chemical
reactions. No movie
theater, no motion

picture, and no
favorite part.

 No oil powered lamp,
and no battery-
operated radio.
No Kerouac, and
no vagabond shoes.
No beat generation,
and no revolution.
No paper, no blue

ink, and no 2am

philosophies.

No chance taken that

is w/o reason or wrong,

and no mistake.

Loot the museo de

Barcelona. Steal

everything in sight!!'".

Viola put the poem

in her pocket. It

continued to rain.

And together Milo

and Viola stand

in a bus stop

with retrospection.

Act 3

In Bairro Alto.
The words seem to
jump off the page.
He is the protagonist.
Each word is
superimposed onto

the paper as
if by magic.

3am. He folds the
paper in thirds.
In the pocket of
his coat is a poem,
which he carries
with him as if it
were a manual.

A jazz'n club.
Mesa 13. A girl in
a wool beany read
an excerpt from a
memo pad.

"Where are all the
Moon Travellers?
Are they gone, or
are they fashionably
late? Have they saved
their dreams in a

jar? Or do they
have none. . ?"

The music began
w/ an offbeat.
Then the bass.

The excerpt left a
mark on everyone in
the room. There was
magic in the air.

I had a cigarette.
The show was on.

Dissolve to: Bairro
Alto. I ambled into
the night, from Rua
do Norte onto the
cafés on Rua Augusta.

The cafés had closed.
There was a taxi on
Dona Maria. No one

was there except

for me and the moon.

I laid down under

the construction

paper stars.

  I found a euro

on the floor.

Another wasted

wish, I thought.

I decided then

that wishes don't

expire, so I saved
the euro for
another time.

**Per-chance a dream,
a word picture.**
Madrid can be seen
from a distance.
Many stars dot the
stratosphere. One

star is brighter
than the others,
as some stars are.

A romantic, all
in on making a
mistake, because
some shoes are made
for walking, and
because the purpose
of the flower,
is the flower.

Dissolve to: *En un
tren a Madrid*, and a
girl in denim blue
Levi's, off to
save the world.

On Super 8, and in
24 frames per second.
On a blueprint, a
transistor radio, and
an almost full moon.

I had a cola in a
bar on Rua da Rosa.
I began to record an
idea, a 300 word hello
la Luna I could fold
in thirds and send
a girl in Spain on a
portable typewriter,
in a room w/ a poster
where I burned the
midnight oil, in summer

when the air is even

more blue, at night

on the roof of a

theater where a

regular superhero was

suspected of gluing

poems on bus stops,

when ten thousand

disobedient dreamers,

all in on fiction,

marched in opposition
to normal ideas.

 Words on paper,
I exaggerated
everything, and
as in art, I was
in front of life.

In a Mercedes-Benz

Taxi. *Rua do Norte.*

A protestor set flyers

off from a cannon.

Paper appeared to

fall from space. I

had one more exposure.

The driver had the

radio on. And so it

may be said, that we

were in a confetti
paper supernova.

I paused for a
picture on the roof
of the car, as if I
was in a movie. On
paper, and in blue ink,
one day a footnote in
a divine melodrama.

In turn, an outline
is had, and from it
another generation
has something that
it can call its own.

Then like fiction,
in a second-floor
apartment, a Kodak
Super 8 film print

flickers through a
projector, 24 frames
per second, and like
magic, made the
illusion of movement.

Other poems by
Mat de Melo,
Fiction Inc., 2024

Follow the subculture,
matdemelo.info

Write to us
nova ink printhouse
novainkprinthouse
@proton.me